The Owl Who Lost Its Twoo

Suzie Allkins

O llie is an owl
with a very tiny beak,
but something MASSIVE happens
when he begins to speak.

His cheeks turn different
colours~shades of red and blue,

until out comes

the loudest ever

TWIT T-WOO!

Wise Old Wizard Owl
appeared one moonlit night.

"What's all this noise?" he asked
(with his wings crossed
firm and tight).

"Ollie!" cried the foxes.

"Ollie!" squeaked the mice.

"He's shouting all the time
and we don't think it's very nice!"

The Wizard Owl listened
to all they had to say.

"Thank you for your time
but now I must be on my way."

He glided through the midnight sky
    with grace and elegance
and found a noisy Ollie
    perched upon a farmyard fence.

He greeted little Ollie
    with a flapping of his wing,
then waved his wand in circles
    whilst he began to sing.

"Noisy~doo and noisy~dee,
    twiddle diddle~doo
Shushy~doo and shushy~dee,
    no more Twit T~woo."

A boom as loud as thunder
echoed on the breeze,
and the brightest
greens and purples
started flashing
through the trees.

Ollie's knees began to wobble
and he landed in a heap.
He felt his eyelids start to close
and soon he was asleep.

He woke up with a smile and thought
'What a funny dream.'
(With no idea that things
were not quite as they did seem.)
Ollie stretched his wings
and flew into the wood,

then sat up high,
feeling proud,
like all good owls should.

A mouse!
A mouse, collecting a cone!

"Hooray!" thought Ollie,
"I am not alone."

He splayed his claws

and gripped the branch tight...

and...

TWIT TWIT!

travelled into
the night!

The mouse looked up and said
"Do you mind?
To call me names like that
isn't very kind."

Ollie was amazed and thought
   "What can I do?
It seems to be apparent
   that I have lost my t~woo!"

"How very strange,"
   Ollie mused,
"I must try again."

When out came a fox
from the inside of its den.

A fox!
  A fox, digging by a tree.
"Yippee!" thought Ollie,
  "I have company."

He breathed in deep
  and puffed out his chest...

and...

TWIT TWIT!

made its way
from nest
to nest!

The fox looked up and said
"Do you mind?
To call me names like that
isn't very kind."

Ollie was upset
   and thought
"If only fox knew
   that somehow
I've been careless
   and mislaid my t~woo!"

"Where *is* my t~woo?"
   the owl cried.
"It needs to come back soon."

When along came a bat
into the light of the moon.

A bat!
   A bat, flying past a tree.
"Woohoo!" thought Ollie,
   "He can speak with me."

He perked up his ears
   then held the bat's stare...

and...

TWIT
TWIT!

resounded
through
the air.

The bat looked up and said
"Do you mind?
To call me names like that
isn't very kind."

Ollie was distraught and thought
    "Bat doesn't have a clue
that I have definitely
    misplaced my t~woo."

Ollie turned away
    and a tear fell from his eye.
He didn't want to speak like this.
    It made him want to cry.

He thought it best
    to hide away and
not say one more word.

It wasn't good
    to be known as
the noisy *and* rude bird!

The fox, the mouse and bat
   decided something must be done
and summoned up the help
   of the Old Wise One.

"Oh dear,"
   the Wizard Owl exclaimed,
"I didn't do it right."
   Then bid his farewells
before he hastily took flight.

It only took one hour
    for Ollie to be found.
He was hiding in a log
    that was lying on the ground.

"I'm sorry," said the Wizard Owl,
    "my spell has gone all wrong.
        Perhaps you'll let me put it right?
        It won't take very long."

    "But before I do," the Wise Owl said,
        "you must promise me
            that if I help to find your t~woo,
            you'll speak more quietly."

Ollie nodded in agreement
    and the Wizard cast his spell.
(Thankfully for Ollie,
    this time it worked quite well!)

Ollie learned his lesson,
    now he speaks and doesn't yell
and thinks about the words he says
    (as they can hurt as well).
Although he knows he mustn't shout
    or shriek or holler too,

when no one seems
to be around,
he still enjoys a big...

AUTHOR AND ILLUSTRATOR

Suzie Allkins lives in Christchurch, Dorset, with her husband and two young children. She was a primary school teacher for many years before embarking upon the creation of her own children's stories. She feels lucky to have been in a job that allowed her to see how children can become wonderfully absorbed into a fictional world by simply picking up a book. Suzie now hopes to encourage this love of reading further through stories and illustrations which offer a message, yet also bring a smile!

For Mum – always with me

suzieallkins@suzieallkins.com

Printed in Great Britain
by Amazon

76735684R00020